Sea Turtle School

Coral Ripley

Special thanks to Sarah Hawkins
For Lyra Didymus-True

ORCHARD BOOKS

First published in Great Britain in 2020 by The Watts Publishing Group

1 3 5 7 9 10 8 6 4 2

Text copyright © Orchard Books, 2020
Illustrations copyright © Orchard Books, 2020

A CIP catalogue record for this book
is available from the British Library.

ISBN 978 1 40836 002 6

Printed and bound in Great Britain by Clays Ltd, Elcograf S.p.A.

The paper and board used in this book are made from wood from responsible sources.

Orchard Books
An imprint of
Hachette Children's Group
Part of The Watts Publishing Group Limited
Carmelite House
50 Victoria Embankment
London EC4Y 0DZ

An Hachette UK Company
www.hachette.co.uk
www.hachettechildrens.co.uk

Contents

Chapter One

"Welcome to the Mermaid Café!" Emily said cheerfully as the bell on the door gave a friendly jangle and a family came in. She looked around the busy café, full of chattering customers. "You can sit there," she said, pointing to a table in front of the window. It was one of her favourite spots because you could see down the hill, past the pastel-coloured

shops and houses, and all the way to the sparkling blue sea.

Emily grinned. She didn't think she would ever get tired of seeing the sea from her house! She and her parents had moved to Sandcombe, to the flat above the café, from a big city a few months ago. When her dad had lost his job her parents had decided to follow their dream of having a seaside café and Emily was so glad they had! Everyone had fallen in love with Mum's delicious cakes and Dad's frothy coffees, and the Mermaid Café was a huge success.

A table of ladies who came in every Saturday morning for their knitting club burst into laughter as a ball of bright yellow wool fell off the table and a big, ginger cat pounced on it as it rolled across the floor.

"No, Nemo!" cried Emily, rushing to grab the wool off her pet cat. As she

handed it back to the knitting club ladies, she noticed a mum who was sitting with

her little girl waving her over.

"What's the house special?" the lady asked, when Emily went to take their order. "My elegant lady friend here and I are out for fancy tea and cakes."

The little girl giggled in delight.

"Oh well," said Emily, playing along, "it's *very* fancy – hot chocolate and a mermaid cupcake."

"Can I have that please, Mummy, please?" the little girl begged, forgetting the game.

"Go on then," her mum smiled. "I'll have one too."

"Good choice!" Emily smiled at the little girl, then went over to the kitchen. "Two house specials," she called to her dad.

"I'm on it!" Dad opened the fridge and pulled out two canisters of squirty cream,

twirling them in the air like a juggler.

Emily giggled as she took the mermaid cupcakes out of the glass display case. They were vanilla cupcakes swirled with delicious frosting in all the colours of the rainbow. She put them on a tray as Dad topped the drinks with whipped cream and marshmallows. "Two hot chocolates

 12

and two mermaid cupcakes!" she said, carefully putting them down in front of the customers.

"Wow!" The little girl's eyes lit up when she saw the colourful cakes. "Do you think this is what mermaids really eat, Mummy?"

"Oh, definitely," her mum said, giving Emily a wink.

Emily smiled back, but it wasn't true. Mermaids ate frostberry ice-cream and seaweed stew – she knew, because she'd actually met them!

On her very first day in Sandcombe, Emily and her friends, Grace and Layla, had rescued a dolphin who was stuck in

 13

a net. But Kai was no ordinary dolphin – he was the pet of a mermaid princess! Princess Marina had used her magic to give Emily, Grace and Layla their own sparkling mermaid tails, and taken them to her underwater kingdom. There, to everyone's amazement, mermaid magic had chosen the three human girls to be Sea Keepers. They were the only ones who could stop a horrible siren called Effluvia from taking over the oceans. It was the Sea Keepers' job to find the Golden Pearls before Effluvia did and use their magic for good instead of evil.

Emily glanced at her purple shell bracelet. As soon as it glowed, it would

be time for another mermaid adventure.
The café door dinged again and with
a jolt Emily stopped daydreaming. She
went behind the counter and helped Dad
pack a Cornish pasty and a salad into a
plastic takeaway box. The next customer
ordered two takeaway teas. Emily pressed
the lids on tight and took their money.

The till had
just closed
when the café
door dinged
again. "Hi,
Emily!" a
familiar voice
called. Emily

looked up to see Grace and her grandad.
Grace's long blonde hair was in a neat
plait, and she was wearing jeans and a
blue top with glittery fishes on it. Her
grandad was dressed in a thick blue
jumper and waterproof trousers.

"A cappuccino and five blueberry
muffins to go, please," he asked Emily.

"Five muffins?" Emily asked in surprise.

Grace's grandad sighed. "Everyone on
the fishing boat is addicted to them," he
explained. "If I have one, the whole crew
will want one."

Emily and Grace giggled.

"Are you going fishing too?" Emily
asked Grace. Her friend loved being out

on the sea and even had her own dinghy.

Grace shook her head. "I came to see if you wanted to go to the park. I'm meeting Layla there."

Emily glanced around at the busy café. She *did* want to hang out with her friends, but she couldn't leave her parents short-staffed. "Um, I'm not sure . . ."

"What's that?" Mum came over with the coffee and squeezed the lid on it as Emily bagged up the muffins.

"Grace asked if I can go to the park," Emily said.

"Of course you should go!" Dad said, flicking Emily lightly with a tea towel. "The morning rush is over, and it's a

 17

beautiful day! Go out and enjoy it."

"OK, thanks!" Emily grinned, pulling off her apron and rushing round the counter.

"Can I just get you to do one job first?" Mum asked.

She reached under the glass counter and brought out three mermaid cupcakes. "These need eating up. I don't suppose you girls can help me out with that?"

"That's the sort of job that we are *very* good at!" Emily joked.

Waving goodbye to everyone, they ran out of the door, the bell dinging cheerfully behind them. Grace always wanted to run everywhere, and today

 18

Emily didn't mind as they raced down
the hill towards the sea. Seagulls were
squawking overhead, she had a mermaid
cupcake in each hand, and the sun was
warm on her face.

When they
got to the
park, Layla
was swinging
on a swing
and looking
out to sea.
Emily waved
the cupcake
in Layla's face
and laughed

as her friend's eyes grew wide when she saw the sweet treat. But it wasn't just the delicious cake that had made Layla excited . . .

"Look!" she said, grabbing Emily's hand. Her shell bracelet was glowing – and so were Grace and Layla's. It was

time for another mermaid adventure!

They set their mermaid cupcakes down next to the swings. No time would pass here while they were gone, so they could eat their snacks when they got back.

Then they held hands and said the magic words Marina had taught them:

"Take me to the ocean blue,
Sea Keepers to the rescue!"

Blue light swirled around them, making the seagulls nearby squawk and flap. Shimmering magical bubbles surrounded the girls, then suddenly they were swimming in deliciously warm water!

Emily glanced around and spotted a mermaid with wavy hair as colourful as the mermaid cupcakes' icing.

"Welcome to the Caribbean!" said Princess Marina.

Chapter Two

Emily, Grace and Layla swam round in delight. They were mermaids again! Emily reached down and touched her tail. It was covered in glittering golden scales the size of her littlest fingernail, and the flippers were light pink. "I've always wanted to go to the Caribbean," she told Marina excitedly. "My birth mother was Afro-Caribbean. Mum and

Dad have always said that we can go there one day."

"Oh, that's amazing!" Layla said.

"Do you mind being adopted?" Grace asked.

Emily thought for a second, then shook her head. She had been adopted when she was tiny, so she didn't remember her birth mother at all. "Sometimes it makes me sad that my birth mum couldn't look after me," she said. "But I love my mum and dad so much. If I wasn't adopted, I wouldn't have them, or Nemo, and I wouldn't have met you and got to be a mermaid!" She swirled her tail through the blue water. Shafts of sunshine pierced

through the surface and it was lovely
and warm, like being in a bubble bath.
The seabed was strewn with lush green
seaweed and anemone-covered rocks,
and there were colourful fish everywhere,
darting through the clear waters. Emily

watched in delight as a school of zebra-striped fish swam past.

"Why are we here? Has the Mystic Clam remembered where another pearl is hidden?" Grace asked Marina.

Marina nodded, her rainbow hair swirling around as she recited the riddle:

"They live in the sea, but are born on land,

Near their nest you'll find a pearl in the sand."

"It must be a bird," Grace said.

Emily nodded too. "Maybe it's a pelican. There are meant to be lots of those in the Caribbean . . ."

The girls were still puzzling over the

riddle when there was a whooshing noise
from high above them. They looked
up to see a giant humpback whale
breaching at the surface. As it dived
back down, they saw lots of sea creatures
sitting on its back. "A whale bus!"
Layla exclaimed, remembering the one
they'd seen in Atlantis on their very first
adventure.

Layla, Emily and Grace grinned as
they watched the magnificent whale
swim past. When it got closer, they could
see that all the creatures riding it were
sea turtles, with greeny-brown shells and
speckled flippers.

"I've always wanted to see a sea turtle!"

 27

Emily squealed with excitement.

"Well, now you've seen a whole bus full of them!" Layla joked.

"That's the bus to sea turtle school," Marina told them. "The Caribbean mermaids run it."

"Wait for me!" a little voice squeaked. A young sea turtle was swimming after the whale bus as fast as he could. But he was never going to catch up with the huge whale. As it sped away, the turtle watched it go and gave a big sigh.

Emily and the others exchanged a glance and swam over to him.

"Are you OK?" Emily asked.

"I'm going to be in *so* much trouble," the little turtle said. "I missed the bus and I'll be late for school. And I don't have anything for show and tell." He looked down at his flippers sadly. "My friend Alisha has something really cool to show but I don't have *anything*." He gave another shell-shaking sigh.

"Maybe we can help," Layla said. "I'm Layla, this is Emily, Grace and Princess Marina. We're the Sea Keepers."

The little turtle looked at them with big eyes. "Wow! Hi! I'm Logan. I never thought I'd meet you. My friends will never believe this." The turtle gasped. "I know! Will you come with me to school? You can be my show and tell! No one's ever brought a Sea Keeper to school before – or a princess. Please? Pretty please with seaweed on top?" He looked at them with his eyes pleading and wide.

Marina and the girls grinned at each other. The little sea turtle was so cute!

He had a green shell and a lovely brown
pattern, almost like the patches on a
giraffe, over his face and flippers.

"We *could* ask the Caribbean mermaids
about the riddle?" Grace suggested.

"I'd love to see more turtles," Emily
added.

"And since you asked so nicely . . ."

 31

Layla said with a grin.

"Let's go!" Marina said, nodding.

"Yes!" Logan celebrated. "Let's do it or we won't get there before the shell goes!"

They followed the little turtle as he sped along, passing fish of all sizes and colours. Emily jumped when she saw a huge pair of black eyes peering out of the seaweed at her, but then the fish moved and she realised the eyes were actually two spots on its back. "Morning, Sea Keepers," the fish said in a deep voice.

"Those are the sea caves where my auntie lives." Logan gave them a tour while they swam. As they went past the sea caves, the girls peeked inside.

"I wish we could explore!" Grace said.

Emily was secretly glad they couldn't stop. The sea caves looked a bit creepy!

Finally, Logan led them through a curtain of bubbles that whooshed and popped around them like they were in a washing machine. "My school's just through here."

"Mermaid magic," Layla whispered excitedly to her friends. Mermaids often used magical bubbles to keep their world hidden from humans.

"There it is," Logan said proudly as the bubbles cleared. He pointed with his flipper to an upturned boat resting on the sandy seabed. It was painted sunshine

 33

yellow and bright blue and had woven seaweed fences all around it.

As Logan led them towards the gate, there was a loud noise. A beautiful mermaid was blowing into a shell. She had an orange tail and plaited black hair that was twisted high on her head.

"We made it in time!" Logan grinned and beckoned them inside. "Come on!" They joined the crowd of young turtles swimming into the boat.

Inside, a whole class of sea turtles about Logan's age were settling down on the sandy seabed. Logan high-finned the other turtles as he took his place at the back. All the turtles started talking

at once when they noticed the four
mermaid visitors sitting next to him.

"All right, settle down," a firm voice
said. The mermaid from earlier swam in,
clapping her hands. When she saw the
girls and Marina at the back of the class
she gasped in surprise. "Oh! Hello!" She
dipped her head and bobbed in the water.
"What an honour, Your Highness."

"Hello," Marina said. "We're Logan's

show and tell," she explained in a whisper. "I've brought the Sea Keepers with me."

The mermaid teacher laughed. "Well, Logan always does like to do things a little differently! My name is Calypso. It's a pleasure to have you here."

She swam to the front of the class and clapped her hands again. "So this seems like it's going to be a very exciting show

and tell. Who wants to go first?"

"Me, me, me!" Every little turtle waved their flippers in the air.

Calypso pointed to a small turtle at the front of the class.

"Alisha always gets to go first," Logan grumbled.

Alisha looked very different to Logan, with a pretty black shell speckled all over with white, like the stars in the night sky. "Is she a different type of sea turtle?" Emily whispered.

"She's a leatherback turtle," Marina said, nodding. "There are four types of sea turtle in the Caribbean: loggerhead, green, hawksbill and leatherback.

They're all really endangered, which is why the mermaids set up this school to look after the little ones."

Alisha swam up to the front of the class and showed everyone a pretty purple shell she'd found. "My grandma says it's really rare," she boasted. The class clapped politely.

"Who cares about a boring old shell!" Logan whispered to them.

"Shhhhhh!" Layla giggled. "Be nice."

"Now, let's have Oria," Calypso called.

The next turtle looked different again. She was brown and speckled like Logan, but her pattern was darker, and her mouth was pointed, like a bird's beak. "Is

 39

she a hawksbill?" Emily guessed.

Marina nodded.

"What have you brought to show us, Oria?" Calypso asked.

"This bendy toy!" Oria held it up proudly.

Emily gasped. It was a plastic straw, like the ones they had in the café!

Calypso looked worried as well. "That isn't a toy, it's very, very dangerous,"

she said, taking the straw and holding it up. "Everyone, make sure you stay away from these. They can get stuck in your nose and stop you from breathing. Oria, you were very lucky that it didn't hurt you."

Oria looked upset and Calypso gave her a hug. "It's actually a good thing you brought it in, because now everyone in the class knows not to go near these horrible things."

"They're called straws," Layla explained. "They're from the human world."

"What do we do if we see a straw?" Calypso asked the class.

"Stay away," they chorused.

"Good. Now maybe Logan can introduce his guests and they can tell us a bit more about the human world."

 41

Logan swam to the front of the class. "I've brought Princess Marina and the Sea Keepers!" he said proudly.

All the turtles gasped except Alisha, who pretended to yawn. Logan stuck his tongue out at her.

Emily followed her friends to the front. She hated being the centre of attention, but she wanted to help Logan. Luckily, Layla loved performing and being in the spotlight, so she swam forward and talked to all the little turtles.

"We're the Sea Keepers!" Layla said. "Do you have any questions for us?"

"Are you really humans?" asked a little loggerhead turtle.

"Yes," said Emily. "But we turn into mermaids thanks to our magic bracelets." She showed the sea turtles the purple shells around her wrist.

"Are you going to stop Effluvia?" a small green turtle said.

Grace nodded. "Our job is to find the Golden Pearls before Effluvia can. We've already found three!" she said.

Every single turtle put their flipper up, and Logan looked proud as the Sea Keepers answered question after question.

"Just time for one more question," Calypso said.

"Why do humans put things like straws in the sea?" Alisha asked.

"Do they want to hurt us?" one of the hawksbill turtles said sadly.

"Yes, why?" One by one all the little turtles joined in.

Emily, Grace and Layla looked at each other in dismay. What could they say?

Chapter Three

The little turtles stared at the girls expectantly, waiting for an answer.

"People aren't trying to hurt you," Layla said finally. "They don't think that their rubbish is going to end up in the sea. But it does."

"Well, you should tell them!" Logan said. The other turtles nodded.

"We will," Emily promised.

 45

Calypso clapped her hands again. "I think that's enough questions," she said. "Would you like to see the rest of the school?"

"Yes, please!" Grace said.

"Right, class, Miss Briareus is going to help you get on with your alphabet while I show the Sea Keepers around," Calypso said.

A red- and white-speckled octopus came into the class and swam up to the front. "Say goodbye, class," she told them.

"Bye, bye!" The little turtles waved with their flippers.

"Thank you for helping me," Logan

said, swimming up to give them each a hug goodbye. "My show and tell was *so* much better than Alisha's," he added with a grin.

Calypso swam through the boat with the girls and Marina following her. "This is where the youngest turtles sleep," she said, letting them peek into a room full of bunk beds. "And this is our canteen," she said, taking them into a room with the ship's wheel in it. All around, young turtles were sitting on benches and eating plates piled high with seaweed curry. It smelled delicious!

"And this is my favourite room," Calypso grinned, taking them through the canteen, to the very back of the boat. The boat curved overhead to make a cosy, sunshine-yellow ceiling and the floor was the softest white sand. Another mermaid teacher with curly black hair and a golden tail was decorating the wooden walls with pretty shells.

"This is the nursery," Calypso said. "Tanice looks after the youngest turtles."

 48

Tanice waved to the girls happily. "I love my job, the babies are so cute!" she said with a grin.

"Where are they?" Grace asked, looking around.

"They haven't arrived yet," Calypso told her. "But it's almost time for them to hatch, so we're busy getting ready."

Emily was about to ask more questions when the shell sounded again. "Play time!" Calypso said cheerfully. The boat rocked from side to side as all the turtles swam outside.

They went out to the seaweed-fenced playground. There were collages pinned round it, a starfish and whale bus made out of shells, and even a picture made out of driftwood and seaweed that showed a family of mermaids . . .

"Is that you, with King Caspian and Queen Adrianna?" Grace asked Marina.

"It is! They've even got Prince Neptune's smug smile!" Layla joked.

"And Marina's beautiful rainbow hair!" Emily said, pointing at some purple seaweed.

But best of all, the playground was full of turtles having fun!

"The turtles are so sweet," Marina said, smiling.

Miss Briareus the octopus had gone into the middle of the playground and

was giving the turtles rides on each of
her eight legs, like a roundabout. In one
corner of the playground turtles were
playing noughts and crosses with starfish
and urchins in the sand.

"Sea Keepers!" Logan rushed over to
them. "Do you want to play dolphin in

the middle? You can be the dolphin, I don't mind!"

"I'd love to play with you," Grace grinned.

"I want to try out the octopus-about!" Layla said. While Marina and Calypso chatted, the girls swam out into the playground with all the laughing turtles.

Emily was happy to just watch, but a little hawksbill turtle tugged on her tail. "Want to play noughts and crosses?" she asked shyly.

"With you? Yes, please," Emily said kindly.

When the hawksbill nudged a sea urchin with her nose, Emily carefully

 53

picked up a wriggly starfish to make her move.

"Sorry!" she said as she lifted it up.

"Put me in the top right!" the starfish whispered.

"Thanks!" Emily giggled.

The little turtle was just about to win when there was the sound of the shell being blown – very badly. Everyone put their hands and flippers over their ears.

The girls turned to see a mermaid with a dark purple tail and blue-black hair at the entrance to the playground. Next to her, an angler fish with a light hanging over his eyes was going bright red as he blew into a shell.

"Enough!" Effluvia snapped. Fang stopped and gasped for breath.

"Well, isn't this sweet," Effluvia drawled. "But I'm afraid play time is over."

Next to Emily, the little loggerhead turtle was shaking. "It's OK," Emily said, bending down to comfort her.

Just then there was a scream from across the playground. "Look at her comb!" Alisha shrieked.

Pinning back Effluvia's long blue-black hair was a speckled brown comb. Emily scrunched up her eyes as she looked from Alisha to the comb. "Is that . . ."

"Tortoiseshell," Calypso said grimly as

 55

she and Marina came and joined Emily.

Calypso clapped her hands and all the turtles swam over to her. Grace and Layla came too, herding the young turtles to safety.

"How dare she!" Marina said furiously.

Effluvia put her hand to her comb and gave a tinkling laugh. "I see you've noticed my new comb," she sneered. "Maybe I'll use *your* shells to make matching jewellery for my siren sisters!"

The little turtles shrieked in fear and hid behind Calypso and the girls.

"We won't let that happen," Grace said firmly.

"You two-legs won't be able to stop

56

me!" Effluvia crowed.
"Once I get a Golden
Pearl my sisters and
I will rule the seas."
Effluvia caught sight
of the collage of the
royal family and
ripped it down. "You'd
better start making
pictures of *me*!" And
with a wicked laugh,
she tore it apart,
the seaweed and
driftwood floating
away through the
water.

 57

Emily thought fast. Maybe if Effluvia believed they'd given her a clue where the pearl was she'd go away. "Follow my lead," she whispered to her friends. Layla and Grace nodded.

"You won't get the Golden Pearl," she said as loudly as she could. "You'll never get to the sea caves before us—" Emily gasped and put her hands over her mouth, pretending she'd made a horrible mistake.

Effluvia stopped ripping the artwork and turned to her, a horrible gleam in her eye.

"Did you hear that, Effluvia? She said the sea caves. That must be where the

 58

next pearl is!" Fang
flapped his fins
excitedly.

"Emily, how
could you?" Layla
said crossly. For
a second Emily
worried that her friend really *was* angry
with her – Layla was such a good actor!

"She said the sea *waves*," Grace added,
getting into it.

"She said *caves*!" Effluvia grinned
nastily. "And that's where I'll go. Come
on, Fang!" She sang a high note, then
she and Fang disappeared in a swirl of
magical bubbles.

"Phew!" Emily breathed a sigh of relief.

"Good thinking!" Grace grinned. "That ought to keep her busy for a while."

Emily nodded. "But meanwhile we need to work out where the Golden Pearl *really* is – and fast!"

Chapter Four

The young sea turtles looked at the girls with worried eyes. "Don't worry, the Sea Keepers will fix everything!" Logan declared.

"Yes, we will," Emily agreed, sounding more confident than she felt. "But first we need to solve a riddle."

"What was it again?" Layla asked the others. "Something about a nest?"

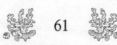

"They live in the sea, but are born on land. Near their nest you'll find a pearl in the sand," Grace recited.

"Oh, I know, I know!" called Alisha.

"Me too, I know, PICK ME!" Logan waved his flipper as high as he could.

"You do?" Emily asked in surprise.

All the little turtles swam in front of the girls, their fins stretched high.

 62

"Why, yes," Calypso laughed. "Isn't it obvious?"

"No!" Grace said. "But it's amazing that you know it – what is it?"

"Right, class, all together," Calypso said.

"Sea turtles!" the turtles said, bursting into laughter.

"Sea turtles?" Layla said in disbelief. "I never would have guessed that!"

"They live in the sea, but they go on land to lay their eggs," Calypso explained. "The mother turtle crawls up on to the beach and buries her eggs in a nest under the sand and leaves them there. About six weeks later, the babies hatch and then they race into the sea as fast as they can."

"I bet I was faster than you," Alisha whispered to Logan.

"Were not," Logan replied.

Emily knew lots about animals, but she didn't know that. She'd thought only birds had nests!

"The hatchlings wait until night time, then make their way to the sea, guided by the moon and the sound of the waves," Calypso told them. "But it's a very dangerous journey, and not all the babies make it."

"Why is it so dangerous?" Layla asked.

"Well, the baby turtles have to get to

the sea, but they are easily confused by loud noises or bright lights. Humans have put lights near the beaches and the baby turtles sometimes end up going the wrong way," Calypso explained.

Oh no! Emily couldn't bear to think about the tiny turtles getting lost because of humans.

"And there are lots of predators too," Calypso added. "Seabirds, fire ants and crabs all like eating turtle hatchlings if they get the chance."

Emily reached out and gave Logan a hug. "You're squishing me!" the little turtle complained, squirming away.

"Sorry!" Emily laughed. She was just

 65

so glad that he and the other turtles had made it safely to the sea turtle school.

"So the Golden Pearl is near a sea turtle nest. But that could be anywhere!" Grace said.

Calypso shook her head. "They always go to the same beaches to lay their eggs. We call it Sea Turtle Island – and best of all there are no humans there, so it's safe for mermaids to go there too. We'll make you a map, come on, class!"

Quickly, the turtles gathered seaweed, driftwood and shells, and soon they'd collaged a map on the seabed.

Grace stared at the picture as she tried to memorise the route. "So we go east

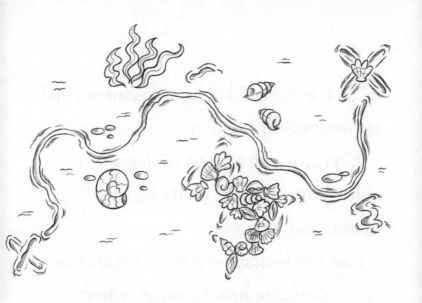

until we get to a big rock shaped like a hammerhead shark?" she said. "And then if we go to the surface we should be able to see the island."

Calypso nodded. "I wish I could come, but I have to stay here with my students," she said.

"You've been a huge help already," Marina told her.

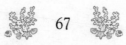

"You all have!" Layla said, and the sea turtles grinned proudly.

"Come on – it won't take long for Effluvia to work out we tricked her!" Emily said nervously.

The Sea Keepers waved to the turtles and set off through the warm waters. There were so many amazing tropical fish to look at, it was like swimming through an aquarium.

"Look!" Layla pointed out a crowd of bright yellow fish.

"They're butterflyfish," Marina told them.

"That one's even more colourful," Emily said, spotting a sparkly multicoloured fish darting amongst the weeds.

"That's a rainbow parrotfish," Marina said. "They can live up to sixteen years old."

Finally, Grace spotted the shark rock. "There it is!" she called out. It really did look like a hammerhead shark.

"We should be nearly there," Marina said.

"I'll go to the surface and see if I can see the island!" Grace said. She swam on ahead, while Emily, Marina and Layla swam along behind.

Emily wondered if Effluvia was still searching the sea caves. It wouldn't be long before she worked out the girls

 69

had tricked her – but they had to stop her from getting the Golden Pearl. She thought about how horrible Effluvia had been to the lovely sea turtles and felt a wave of determination. They were going to stop her, no matter what!

"Help!" a voice called from up ahead. "Please help!"

Layla turned to Emily, her eyes wide. "Quick! Grace is in trouble!"

Chapter Five

They swam up to the surface as fast as they could. As they got closer, the water became murky and filled with colourful bits. *What is this?* Emily wondered – but there was no time to stop – Grace needed their help!

"Oh phew!" Grace said when the others arrived. "I'm stuck!" She thrashed her tail, which was tangled in a huge mess.

Emily, Layla and Marina gasped as they swam up close. Grace was trapped by a huge island – made of rubbish!

"What is all this?" Grace asked.

There were nets and floating buoys, tangled up with what looked like a plastic washing basket, netting and hundreds of plastic bottles – ones that

had had water or fizzy drinks in, the kind Emily saw every day at home. She saw a plastic cup like the ones they used in the café. And lids too. She could hardly bear to look at it.

"Hold still, we'll get you out," Marina said.

She dived underwater. Emily and Layla followed. It was just as messy there as it was on the surface. It was a bit like Layla's bedroom when she emptied everything on to her bedroom floor and they had to wade through it to get to her bed. Except Layla's messy bedroom couldn't hurt anyone.

"It's like a rubbish dump, but why

is it in the middle of the sea?" Layla
wondered out loud.

"It's all plastic," Emily said. There
was a takeaway box, like the ones they
always got takeaways in on Friday
nights. A cotton bud floated past. A
seahorse was trying to cling on to it with
his tail. Emily gently caught it with her
hands cupped. "That's no good, let me
help you," she told it.

The tiny
seahorse blinked
up at her. Emily
dived down to
the seabed and
found a patch of

seaweed. She opened her hand and the seahorse caught the weed with its tail, clinging on.

Emily swam back up to join Marina and Layla, who were still trying to untangle Grace's tail.

"Tell Grace we'll have her free in a minute," Marina said.

Emily went back to the surface. Grace was looking about miserably.

"There's a toothbrush over there," she said. "And a plastic fork. I used a plastic fork yesterday when Mum and I got fish and chips after my swimming lesson." Emily didn't know what to say. She used plastic things all the time. Sometimes she just used them once, then put them in the recycling bin. She never thought they might end up here.

"You're free!" Layla and Marina popped their heads above water.

"It's just horrible," Emily said, feeling close to tears. "And it's so big." The mess stretched out as far as they could see on the horizon.

"I've heard about these garbage islands," Marina said. "There are five or six of them, all as big as this. They're made when litter gets caught in swirling currents and it gathers together."

Some seagulls were flying down and pecking at the detritus on the surface.

76

"Go away!" Emily yelled. She didn't want them getting hurt.

"Come on, let's go find the real island," Grace said.

They dived underneath the water, swimming under the rubbish. All around them bits and pieces of plastic of various colours floated by. It was like swimming in a bin, or a soup. There were milk-bottle tops and toothbrushes and lots of tiny bits of colourful plastic like confetti bobbing in the water. They swam along in silence, looking at everything they passed.

Emily watched a plastic bag floating along. It was from the supermarket her family always went to. What was it doing here, thousands of miles away? She watched as it bobbed along – and behind it was a sea turtle, its mouth open wide.

"Stop!" Emily yelled. "Don't eat that!"

Kicking her fins, she swam forward and snatched the plastic bag just in time.

"HEY! Get your own jellyfish," yelled

the turtle. She was a huge leatherback, almost as big as Emily's dad.

"It's not a jellyfish!" Emily gasped.

"Are you sure?" The turtle looked at it. Filled with water and bobbing along on the tide, the bag really did look like a jellyfish. Emily scrunched up the plastic so that the turtle could see.

"Oh, well then, thanks," the turtle said.

"It's a really easy mistake to make," Marina told her.

"You should swim somewhere safer," Grace said. "And tell all your friends to be careful."

"I will," the turtle said gratefully. "Thanks. I'm so glad I met you. If there's

 79

ever anything I can do for you, just let me know . . ."

"Do you know where Sea Turtle Island is?" Layla asked.

"It's just over there." The turtle pointed a flipper.

"Thanks!" the girls said. They went back to the surface and looked the way the turtle had pointed.

Pulling her wet hair out of her face, Emily squinted in the bright sunshine.

"I can see some palm trees!" Layla yelled. "We're almost there!"

The water turned a beautiful light blue as they got closer to the island. "Soon it will be shallow enough for us to walk!"

Grace said with a grin.

"This is going to be the easiest pearl yet!" Layla grinned.

The water was so shallow now that Emily could hardly swim without hitting the sandy seabed with her tail. "Can you turn us back into humans, Marina?" she asked.

"Not so fast, *two-legs*!" a horribly familiar voice called. Effluvia swam up behind them, looking furious. "You thought you could fool me – well, you didn't."

"There's nothing you can do to stop us, Effluvia! We can go on to the island and you can't!" Grace said.

 81

"Oh, we'll *sea* about that," Effluvia spat. "If I can't have the pearl, no one can!" She threw back her head and opened her mouth. Emily, Grace, Layla and Marina immediately put their hands over their ears. Effluvia had tried to enchant them with her powerful song before. But this time she just let out a high note that pierced the waves and reverberated in the water around them. Suddenly, the shallow water in front of them was filled with . . .

"More plastic bags?" said Layla in confusion.

Emily stared at them and realised that they were moving, and they had trailing tentacles. "No," she said, "those actually are jellyfish. And their stings can really hurt."

"You see," Effluvia laughed, "I told you, it's no good. You might as well give up now!" Effluvia dived under the surface, laughing as she went.

 83

"We'll never give up!" Emily said. But they were completely surrounded by jellyfish. What were they going to do?

Chapter Six

The jellyfish bobbed all around them in the water. It was so amazing to see them up close. With their see-through bodies, they really did look like they were made out of jelly. But under each body, almost invisible in the water, they had trailing tentacles, and Emily knew if she brushed up against one it would hurt a lot. They were like stinging nettles, but worse!

"They're getting closer," she said anxiously.

The girls clustered together as the jellyfish surrounded them.

"Maybe we can talk to them?" Layla suggested. "Hello? Um, excuse me?"

But the jellyfish just bobbed nearer.

"We're running out of room!" Marina said as they backed into each other.

"If only there was a sea turtle here to eat them up!" Grace moaned.

"That's it!" Marina exclaimed in excitement. "Sea turtles aren't the only creatures who like eating jellyfish."

She waved her arms in the water and, despite the danger, the girls grinned.

 86

Marina was going to do mermaid magic!
Colourful bubbles swirled in the water
around them as Marina sang:

"Mermaid magic, hear my plea,
Please send Kai right here to me!"

There was a sudden burst of bubbles,
and when they cleared Marina's dolphin
pet was there – and just in time, because
the jellyfish were almost touching them!

"Kai! The jellyfish are going to sting us,
please help!" Marina called.

Kai clicked in excitement, then swam
towards the nearest jellyfish and gobbled
it up happily.

"Won't they hurt him?" Emily asked.

"No, dolphins don't feel the stings,"

Marina said. "Jellyfish are Kai's favourite snack!"

Kai swam round in circles, gobbling some jellyfish whole and racing after others, herding them like it was a big game. Finally, he chased all the remaining jellyfish away.

The girls breathed a sigh of relief. Kai swam over and Marina hugged him. Emily stroked his smooth back as she said thank you. She still couldn't believe she was friends with a dolphin!

"That was fun!" Kai clicked happily. "What's next?"

"Next we go on the island and look for the pearl!" Grace told him.

"We can get there now, thanks to you,"
Layla added.

They swam through the warm water
right up to the beach, then sat on the
sand, splashing their mermaid tails in the
waves.

"Good luck, girls," Marina said.

Hugging Kai, she sang the song to turn them human again:

"So they can go upon the shore,
Make the girls human once more!"

The water around their tails shimmered, and they turned back into legs. The girls were now dressed in pretty swimming costumes, perfect for the beach. Emily's was a tankini, Grace had shorts and a stripy top and Layla had a swim skirt – and they all matched the colour of their mermaid tails!

Grace jumped up. Layla stood and fell straight over, giggling as Grace ran over to help her. Emily wobbled as her toes sank into the warm sand. It was always strange to get her legs back after being a mermaid!

While Marina and Kai waited in the shallow water, the three girls walked on to the island. It was very different to the beach back home. The water was bright blue and the sand was so pale it was almost white. The sun shone down on them, and Emily could feel the heat sinking into her skin like warm butter melting into toast.

"It's lovely here!" Grace said, doing a cartwheel in excitement.

But just then something caught Emily's eye. An empty plastic water bottle. And further down the beach she could see

 92

a bottle cap and some plastic netting. There might not be any people on this island, but their rubbish was still here.

"Right, we need to find a sea turtle nest . . . where do you think it is?" Layla said, looking at the sand. "It could be anywhere."

Layla was right. Emily had thought there would be some sign that there were turtle eggs buried under the sand, but there wasn't – all the sand looked the same. "I guess the turtle mums don't want predators to know where the eggs are buried in case they eat them," she said thoughtfully.

"But how are we going to find the

 93

Golden Pearl if we can't find the nest?" Layla groaned.

"I guess we'll just have to wait until the turtles hatch. It won't be long until sunset," Grace said, glancing at the horizon.

"And until then, maybe we can clear up the beach and make it safe for the hatchlings to get down to the water!" Emily suggested.

"Good plan!" Layla said.

Grace nodded too, and the three girls started work. It was nice to think that they were helping, and that the plastic they collected wouldn't be washed into the sea to join that horrible island.

Grace found an old bucket and they filled it with rubbish from the beach. There were loads of things half hidden by the sand, and it was fun spotting them and digging them out.

"I wish I could help," Marina called from the water.

"Why don't you sing to us while we work?" Layla suggested.

"OK!" Marina sat on a rock and started to sing. Her beautiful voice was carried by the wind over the gently crashing waves and up to the beach where the girls were still collecting. The sun started to set, painting the sky with brushstrokes of pinks and reds and oranges.

Finally, the beach was clear and the girls scrambled on to the rocks with Marina. They watched the sun set, while Kai splashed about in the water playing fetch with a seashell like an excited puppy.

"Didn't Calypso say that the baby

turtles listen for the sound of the waves?" Layla said.

Emily nodded. "And the light of the moon." Now that it was starting to get dark they could see the moon shining brightly overhead, making the waves sparkle in the moonlight.

"We'd better be really quiet," Layla suggested.

"Shhhh!" Grace said as someone made a rustling noise.

"It's not me!" whispered Layla.

"Or me," Emily said. "It sounds like it's coming from the sand?"

Marina gasped. "I know what it is! The sea turtles are starting to hatch!"

Chapter Seven

Emily watched as the sand high up on the beach started to move and a teeny tiny turtle, the size of her palm, appeared out of the sand. And as the sand shifted, a glowing light shined out. The Golden Pearl!

"Let's wait until the babies have all hatched before we get it," Grace whispered as quietly as she could. "We don't want to disturb them."

"I do!" came a loud voice from the water. There was a ghastly wail and a light started bobbing around.

It was Effluvia, and she was holding

Fang out of the water and using his light like a torch! She aimed the beam of light at the top of the beach like a spotlight, and the baby turtles all started to turn towards it.

"Stop it, you'll confuse the sea turtles!" Layla whispered as loud as she dared.

"Good!" Effluvia shouted.

"Effluvia!" Fang gasped for breath. "I can't breathe! Please! EFFLUVIA!"

"Ugh!" Effluvia huffed in annoyance and dropped him in the water with a *PLOP*. The girls sighed with relief as the baby turtles turned back towards the bright moonlight, shining high over the sea.

But Effluvia wasn't done causing trouble yet. "I can't believe you made it past my jellyfish," she said crossly. "In fact, it's made me really CRABBY."

She sang a low note that echoed around the still beach. For a second, nothing happened, and then some pale shapes started walking sideways out of the water – crabs! They were pale white, and they were making a scary growling noise.

"What are they?" Layla asked. "And what's that spooky noise?"

"Ghost crabs!" Marina told them. "They have teeth in their tummies, and the noise is because they're grinding them. They're hungry."

"That's not all! Tell them what the crabs' favourite food is," Effluvia said, gloating.

Marina looked at the girls sadly. "Sea

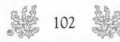

turtle hatchlings!" she said, burying her face in Kai's neck.

More and more crabs came out of the dark water on to the beach. They *did* look like ghosts in the moonlight – a ghostly crab army. And they were heading up the sand, right towards the baby sea turtles!

"We have to get that pearl right now – it's the only way to save the babies!" Emily said, jumping up. She raced up the beach, dodging around the white crabs. One pinched her on the ankle as she ran, and she heard Layla cry out behind her as well, but they all kept going. As they went further up the beach, they passed

tiny turtles heading towards the sea.
Emily carefully tiptoed past them and
dropped to her knees by the nest. There
were still babies scrambling out of it,
and a glow was coming from deep in the
sand. The Golden Pearl had to be down
there somewhere.

 104

"Dig!" Grace said.

They scooped handfuls of sand out of the way. As she dug, Emily glanced down the beach. The sea turtles were pushing themselves over the sand, towards the sea, led by the pull of the moon and the sound of the waves. But the ghost crabs were coming up from the sea, towards them, their tummies still growling hungrily. They had to find the pearl fast or they weren't going to be able to save the sea turtles!

"They're almost at the babies!" Layla cried.

Emily dug even more desperately. Her hand touched something smooth and round. She pulled it out of the sand and was almost blinded by a shimmering light. It was the Golden Pearl!

"Noooooo!" Effluvia shrieked from the water.

"Quick!" Emily gasped.

Layla and Grace's hands landed on

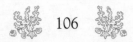

the pearl next to hers so they could use
the magic. On the beach, a crab was
reaching out his pinchers to grab a
hatchling . . .

"I wish the baby turtles were all safely
at the sea turtle school!" Emily said
breathlessly.

The light in the Golden Pearl died

away so it was just a plain white pearl.

"Did it work?" Layla asked. And then with a whoosh, mermaid magic surrounded them and magicked them away.

Chapter Eight

The magic swirled around them, and when they opened their eyes they were mermaids again, and they were back in the playground at the sea turtle school with Marina and Kai.

"Where are the hatchlings?" Emily cried.

"It's OK, they're over there!" Layla pointed to where the tiny sea turtle

babies were floating safely nearby.

Grace sighed in relief. "Phew! That was a close one!"

"Wow!" one of the baby turtles said as he looked at the colourful boat in awe.

Emily hugged her friends happily. They'd beaten Effluvia again and, best of all, the baby turtles were safe!

Just then Calypso and the other turtles noticed them. "Our new class is here!" Calypso said delightedly. "And just in time. The other turtles were just about to go home! Come on, everyone, let's welcome them, just like we practised."

Tanice the nursery mermaid gathered all the newborn turtles up and gave them cuddles while Logan's class lined up in front of them. Logan saw the Sea Keepers and waved his flipper. Emily spotted Alisha and Oria too.

With a nod from Calypso, the sea turtles burst into a happy song, drumming their flippers against their shells to make a funky drum beat as they sang along.

"Welcome to our school,
We hope you think it's cool,
We're going to laugh and play,
As we learn each day,
So welcome, welcome,
Welcome to our school!"

Logan swam over and gave the Sea

Keepers maracas made out of shells
filled with little stones. The girls giggled
as they shook them and joined in the
catchy, happy song.

"Welcome, welcome,

Welcome to our school!"

Finally, the song ended and they burst
into applause.

Calypso blew into the conch shell.
"Time to go inside, little ones," she said
to the babies. "It's bedtime!"

"And I think it's time for you to go
home too," Marina said to the girls.

"Oh," Layla groaned, "but we're having
so much fun!"

"You'll be back again," Marina

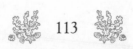

laughed. "I'll let you know as soon as the Mystic Clam remembers where another pearl is."

Layla, Grace and Emily hugged Marina goodbye, and waved to Calypso, but before they could go, all the sea

turtles swam over to them, hugging and high-finning them.

"Bye!" called Alisha.

"Thank you for helping us!" said Oria.

"Come visit us again one day!" Logan said.

Then the turtles gathered next to the mermaids while Marina did the magic that would send the girls home.

"See you soon!" Emily, Grace and Layla called, as magical bubbles surrounded them.

A second later, they were back in the park in Sandcombe, the sun shining down and the sea shimmering in front of them. It was hard to believe that they'd just been underwater, having an amazing mermaid adventure.

"Weren't the sea turtles so cute!" Layla exclaimed.

"And the song was so good!" Emily added.

"*Welcome to our school,*" the girls sang together, then burst into laughter.

"Hey!" Grace suddenly stopped and started flapping her arms. The naughty seagull from earlier had snuck over and was eating their mermaid cupcakes! Bits of colourful frosting and chocolate sponge flew everywhere as he pecked at the cakes messily, squawking in delight.

"Oh no, I was really looking forward to

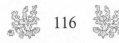

eating that!" Layla said.

"Let's go back to the café, I'm sure Mum will give us more," Emily said.

As they walked back up the cobbled hill, Emily thought about their adventure. It had been fun, but sad too. She couldn't stop thinking about all the plastic they'd seen. It was so awful that plastic lids and cups just like the ones they used at her parents' cafe were floating in the middle of the sea. Some of them could have come from there!

Layla must have been thinking the same thing. "I wish we could do more to help," she said.

"Maybe we can," Emily told her,

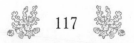

suddenly running on ahead.

"Hey, wait up!" Grace said in surprise, but for once Emily was even faster than she was!

Emily was panting when she burst through the café door with a jangle. She went straight into the kitchen, with Layla and Grace following behind her.

"Hey, what's up?" Dad said when he saw her.

"Plastic cups and lids," Emily said. "They're ending up in the sea. We have to stop using them."

Mum looked at them guiltily. "I know that plastic isn't very good. But we always recycle what we can."

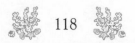 118

"It's not enough." Emily looked at her mum seriously. "We have to stop using it as much as possible."

"Plastic straws are really harmful to sea turtles," Layla chimed in.

"And plastic bags," Grace added. "They think they're jellyfish."

"It's awful that these things litter the planet for hundreds of years," Emily said. "Can't we use non-plastic boxes?" she asked her parents. "Please?"

"We could offer a discount if people bring in reusable coffee cups?" Dad suggested.

"I'll get Grandad to get them for all his crew!" Grace said.

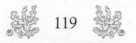

"You feel very strongly about this, don't you, girls?" Mum said.

"If you could see all the rubbish in the ocean, you would too," Emily told her.

"OK. Let's do it!" Mum agreed. "The Mermaid Café is going to be plastic free!"

Emily flung her arms around her mum and squeezed her tight. "Thank you!" she whispered in her ear.

"I'm so proud of you for caring so much about animals," Mum said.

Emily grinned. Mum didn't know it, but it was her job – that's what being a Sea Keeper was all about!

"There's one more thing we need," she added cheekily. "More mermaid cupcakes! A seagull ate ours."

"Hmmm, a likely story!" Dad joked.

"It did!" the girls told him.

"Go on then," Mum said, laughing.

Emily, Layla and Grace each grabbed another cupcake from the counter and ran back outside into the sunshine to eat

 122

them. They sat on the wall outside the café looking down at the glittering sea. Somewhere out there, there was a whole school of sea turtles and – thanks to them – the nursery class was full too.

Emily gave a happy sigh and took a big bite of delicious cake. It wouldn't be long before she was a mermaid again – but until then at least there were mermaid cupcakes!

The End

Join Emily, Grace and Layla
for another mermaid adventure in …

Penguin Island

"Are you done yet?" Layla squirmed as her big sister clipped a huge gold ring to her ear.

"I would be if you'd stop wriggling!" Nadia laughed.

"I can't, I'm too excited!" Layla said, grinning.

"Finished!" Nadia said. "Go and look." Layla ran over to her sister's full-length mirror and laughed out loud. She was dressed like a pirate in shorts and a blue-and-white stripy top. Her dark hair was in a long plait and, as well as the huge earring, Nadia had tied a skull-and-crossbones bandana around her head.

"Just one more thing!" Nadia said, pinning a colourful toy parrot to Layla's shoulder.

Read **Penguin Island** to find out what happens next!

How to be a real-life

Would you like to be a Sea Keeper just like Emily, Grace and Layla? Here are a few ideas for how you can help protect our oceans.

1. Try to use less water

Using too much water is wasteful. Turn off the tap when you brush your teeth and take shorter showers.

2. Use fewer plastic products

Plastic ends up in the ocean and can cause problems for marine wildlife. Instead of using plastic bottles, refill a metal bottle. Carry a tote bag when out shopping, and use non-disposable food containers and cutlery.

Sea Keeper

3. Help at a beach clean-up
Keeping the shore clear of litter means less litter is swept into the sea. Next time you're at the beach or a lake, try and pick up all the litter you can see.

4. Reduce your energy consumption
Turn off lights when you aren't using a room. Walk or cycle instead of driving. Take the stairs instead of the lift. Using less energy helps reduce the effects of climate change.

5. Avoid products that harm marine life
Do not buy items made from endangered species. If you eat seafood, make sure it comes from sustainable sources.

SEA KEEPERS

Dive in to a mermaid adventure!

The Mermaid's Dolphin
Coral Ripley

The Sea Unicorn
Coral Ripley

Coral Reef Rescue
Coral Ripley

Sea Turtle School
Coral Ripley

Penguin Island
Coral Ripley

Coming Soon

Sea Otter Summer Camp
Coral Ripley

The Rainbow Seahorse
Coral Ripley

Whale Song Wedding
Coral Ripley